Ashley's Test

The Bet

Bigmouth

Halloween

Hike

Missing Money

The New Kid

Outdoor Ed Invasion

Shady Neighbors

Vandalism

www.sdlback.com

ISBN-13: 978-1-68021-369-0
ISBN-10: 1-68021-369-5
eBook: 978-1-63078-584-0

Printed in Malaysia

21 20 19 18 17   1 2 3 4 5

Ashley's Test

EVAN JACOBS

Calculus Is Hard!

Mr. Raj often goes off on a tangent.

52. (A) (B) (C) (D)

Nico is smart. He got a perfect score on the SAT.
Five times! (He retakes it for fun.)

slice of ~~piza~~ π
pizza

3.1415926
535897
9323
846
2

Dr. Stefani can't spell, but he's great at
analytic number theory.

Math is like kale. It's good for you, but it
doesn't taste good.

Chapter 1
Math Test

Ashley Moore was always super busy. She represented the sophomore class in student government. Student leaders met at zero period. That was 6:45 a.m. Talking about school events was fun. It woke her up. The next period was math. Calculus. By then she was ready to go.

Ashley was also in Model United Nations. Key Club meetings were every Wednesday at lunch. She ran track for Walden Lane High School too. Being busy was great. She loved it. Her dream after college was law school. Then she wanted a law career.

Mr. Raj taught calculus. He was not in class that morning. Ashley knew he wouldn't be there. The teacher and his wife were expecting. He had missed class a few times already.

Mrs. Smith was the sub. She had taught at the school years ago. She was retired now. But she liked to teach part-time.

There was a test that day. Mrs. Smith was ready. Mr. Raj liked to be there on test day. But he respected Mrs. Smith. She would take the test seriously.

"I didn't study," Darryl Atkins said, laughing. He sat on Ashley's left. Darryl wore his letterman's jacket. He played water polo. His blond hair was buzzed.

"Neither did I," Skylar Martinez said, smirking. Skylar sat in front of Ashley. His head was shaved too. Skylar played on the baseball team.

"Nico," Darryl called. "Did you study, dude?"

Nico Dale looked up from his textbook. He grinned. Nico always dressed preppy. But he didn't play any sports. He just hung out with guys who did.

"Of course," he said.

Mrs. Smith stood in front of the class. "Put everything away, please," she said. She was holding the stack of tests. "You will have the entire period."

A student handed out the tests. Everyone got to work.

Ashley didn't have any trouble. She loved math. Using her brain was fun.

After 20 minutes, she was done. She turned in her test. Mrs. Smith smiled at her.

Then Ashley walked back to her seat. No way! She couldn't believe what she saw. Darryl, Skylar, and Nico were cheating!

Nico finished a problem. He showed the answer to Darryl. Darryl copied it. Then Darryl showed it to Skylar. Nobody noticed. Everyone was focused on their own work. The three boys kept their heads down. It looked like they were working.

Ashley sat down at her desk. She took out some English homework. At one point she looked up. Darryl made eye contact. He had just finished giving Skylar an answer.

Darryl grinned at her.

Ashley went back to her work. But she could feel Darryl's eyes on her.

The bell rang. All the students stopped working. The tests were collected.

Chapter 2
Cheaters

It was lunch. Ashley and Kayla Flores sat on a bench. The campus had a plaza. There was a lot of seating there. Most of the classrooms framed the plaza. The high school was large. It had 2,000 students.

"They were totally taking advantage," Ashley said.

Kayla was looking at Snapchat. "So what?" she said.

Kayla was Ashley's best friend. They'd met in the third grade. Kayla was a sophomore too. But her main focus wasn't academics. She loved theater. NYU was her first-choice college. Ashley was doubtful. Kayla would have to step it up.

The two girls had differences. But they were also very similar. They had long black hair. Ashley's had a bit of curl. Kayla's was stick-straight. The girls dressed alike. They mostly wore T-shirts and jeans. And they were motivated students.

"How can you say that?" Ashley took a bite of pizza. "Cheating is wrong."

"Listen, Miss Lawyer." Kayla put some french fries into her mouth. "Those guys probably cheat all the time. This is just the first time you've noticed."

"I just—it bugs me."

"Well, Amy Richmond bugs me. She

got the lead in *Bye Bye Birdie*. Let it go, Ashley. You have to do that sometimes."

"Maybe you're right." Ashley sighed. She took a sip of water.

"I am, trust me," Kayla said, laughing.

Mrs. Soto was Ashley's AP US History teacher. She was short. Her hair was brown and short. Mrs. Soto was like the color brown. Boring. Frumpy.

"And, Ashley, here's your partner. You'll work with Darryl," Mrs. Soto said.

"Okay," Ashley said.

Darryl got up from his desk. He grinned. It was the same grin he had given Ashley in math. He moved next to her.

Mrs. Soto was teaching about the early 1900s. Everyone had to do a presentation.

They had partners. The report was about a historical figure during that time. Ashley and Darryl had been assigned Carry Nation. She opposed alcohol. Carry Nation had even attacked bars with a hatchet.

"Hey," Darryl said. He took out his cell phone.

The school was big on technology. Students could use their phones in class for schoolwork.

"Looking up Carry Nation?" Ashley asked.

"Not unless she's on Instagram." Darryl laughed.

Ashley stared at him.

"That calculus test was hard," he said.

She was surprised. Why would he bring it up?

"Yeah," Ashley said. She took out her laptop. "Let's find out about Carry Nation."

"I noticed you finished quickly. You turned your test in first."

"I studied," she said.

"I'll bet," Darryl said.

Ashley shot him a look. Then she looked back at her computer.

"Listen," he said. "I just got a job. I'm saving up to buy a car. I was too busy to study. Cheating isn't my thing."

"It's none of my business," she said.

"Cool. It's no big deal." Darryl moved closer. He looked at the computer. "So, who was Carry Nation?"

Chapter 3
Family Talk

The Moore family sat in a booth. They were at Applebee's. It was busy. Most of the tables were full. The family was split on how much they liked the food. Marlon and his dad loved it. Ashley thought it was just okay. Mrs. Moore only liked the salads.

Their looks were split boy-girl too. Ashley's mom had curly short hair. Her eyes were green. Ashley had curly—but not as curly—long hair. She had green eyes too. Both mother and daughter had high cheekbones.

Marlon and his dad had short-short hair. They had dimples. Their eyes were brown.

Their parents had good jobs. Mrs. Moore taught third grade. She also wrote books. It was a hobby. Mr. Moore worked for the city. He planned how the city could handle growth.

"I need a better ending," Ashley's mom said. "The one I have feels wrong."

"Why don't you stop for a bit?" Mr. Moore said. "It couldn't hurt. Maybe you will get some new ideas."

"You're probably right." Mrs. Moore took a sip of iced tea. "This one has been hard."

"I'm having trouble too. Which science experiment should I do?" Marlon asked.

"Maybe I just shouldn't do it. I'll tell the teacher I need to stop for a bit. Get some new ideas."

"Funny, but no," his dad said. "I can help you decide."

"Okay," Marlon said. "I'll show you the list when I get home. But nobody can do the same one. Hopefully the one I pick hasn't been taken."

"How much time have you had?" Ashley asked.

"Two weeks."

"Two weeks?" Ashley rolled her eyes. "Good luck getting anything good now. You're just like the guys in my math class. You wait till the last minute. Then you fail."

"I haven't failed anything." Marlon grinned. "Yet."

"That's your problem," Ashley said. She bit her tongue. Sometimes she could be too critical. People were people. Marlon was different than her. So were Darryl and his friends. "These guys cheated on a test. It was during math. Then I got partnered with one of them for history. I don't want to work with him."

"Well, Ashley," her mom said. "Maybe you'll be a good influence. You never know."

"Yeah," her dad agreed. "Sometimes people want help. The problem is they don't know how to ask for it."

"Or," Marlon said. "He might rub off on you, Ashley. Then I'll be the best student in the family." Marlon wasn't a bad student. He just didn't get good grades on everything. Ashley was driven. Marlon wanted to have fun. He loved video games and movies.

If only that was his homework! He'd be a straight-A student.

"Yeah, right!" Ashley said, laughing.

Her parents smiled.

"I just don't get it," she went on. "These guys are in calculus. They shouldn't have to cheat, right?"

"There are cheaters everywhere," Mr. Moore said.

"It was his attitude," Ashley said.

"You confronted him?" Marlon could not believe it.

"Nope. I didn't have to," Ashley said. "He brought it up in history. He said it was 'no big thing.' "

Chapter 4
Caught

Ashley walked into math the next morning. Instantly she knew something was wrong. Darryl, Skylar, and Nico weren't there. All three were absent. Weird!

She sat down at her desk. Her book was in her backpack. Ashley reached down and grabbed it.

Then she saw Bryce Miller. Bryce was into punk music. He wore a T-shirt for the band Fatal Three. There was a bloody skeleton on it. Ashley never listened to punk. Bryce sat one row up and across from her.

"Somebody told on them," Bryce said. He was talking to another student. "Mr. Raj sent them to the principal."

The bell rang.

Mr. Raj stood in front of the class.

"Let's start. I will return your tests," he said, smiling. "Who wants to help?"

The teacher didn't say a word about the missing students.

Ashley and others raised their hands. She didn't get picked. Mr. Raj chose a student in the front. He divided the stack of tests.

Ashley waited. She looked over at Bryce.

He was looking at her. Bryce didn't

smile. Ashley stared back. He shook his head and looked away.

Whatever! He was strange.

She got her test back. 100 percent! Sweet. She looked up. Bryce was staring at her again.

"Have fun snitching?" he whispered.

Then it hit her. The boys had gotten in trouble for cheating. They thought she told on them.

"You *should* have told on them," Kayla said. "Those guys have been cheating forever."

The girls walked around the campus plaza. They held their phones. Ashley was checking Snapchat. Kayla was texting.

Ashley's eyes darted around. She was looking out for the cheaters. Why was she worried about them? Cheating was wrong.

But she didn't want them to get suspended.

"I thought you didn't care," Ashley said. "You just shrugged your shoulders."

"Yeah, but they finally got caught. Good! Now maybe they will follow the rules. I doubt it, though. Most likely they will be even worse."

"Are they *that* bad?" Ashley asked.

"Yeah, probably," Kayla said. "I don't think they're good."

Ashley didn't agree with her friend. She wasn't close with the boys. But she'd known them since elementary school. Were they bad guys? She'd never thought of them like that.

"Maybe they'll learn something from this," Ashley said.

Kayla stared at her. "Are you from another planet?" she asked.

Chapter 5
Snitch

Ashley sat in Mrs. Soto's class. Her laptop was open. Ashley and Darryl were putting together their report. She showed him a picture. Carry Nation was holding a hatchet. She looked mean. Darryl stared at it. His arms were folded.

"Is this one okay?" she asked.

"Sure," he said, shrugging.

Darryl had been acting odd. He was barely talking. There were no jokes.

"Okay," Ashley said. She smiled.

She put the image into their report. It was due the next week.

"I know you snitched," he said.

Ashley turned. She looked at him. "What?"

"You told Mr. Raj," he said. His tone was stern. "Didn't you? Nah. You probably went straight to the principal."

"Why would I do that?" Ashley asked. "I don't care if you cheat."

"Liar!" he hissed. "You are such a good student. You don't want anybody to do better than you."

"Wait a minute." Her heart pounded. She didn't mind a good debate. But she didn't like finger-pointing. Especially since she didn't do anything! "You told me you cheated. I wasn't the only person there.

Somebody else could have seen you. Maybe they said something."

"Yeah," Darryl said. "It was you. I saw you smile at Mrs. Smith. You probably tell the teachers everything. And you're paid with good grades."

Ashley was pissed. She wanted to yell at him. But no, she wouldn't do that.

It was a stare-down.

"Think what you want." She turned back to her laptop. "We've got work to do."

"Will you tell Mrs. Soto too?" he asked. "I dare you. Tell her I'm not working."

"I won't do it." Ashley looked for more pictures on her laptop. "I didn't snitch. If you want to cheat, do it. That's on you. It's none of my business."

"Yeah, right."

Darryl eventually stood up. He left the classroom.

Ashley thought about talking to Mrs. Soto. It was obvious. She wasn't getting along with Darryl. The teacher would be understanding. But Ashley didn't want more trouble. So she said nothing.

Darryl came back. But he didn't contribute. He just sat behind her. Occasionally he clicked his pen.

Track practice ended around four thirty. She left school with some of the other runners. Their eyes were on their phones.

"Check out Snapchat," Samantha Lee said. "Look, Ashley. What's that all about?"

"What?" Ashley asked.

She opened up Snapchat. Her jaw

dropped. She went completely cold inside. Her heart thumped.

It was a picture of her. She was sitting in Mrs. Soto's class. Her laptop was open. Mean words moved across the image.

SHE WILL SNITCH YOU OUT!

Chapter 6
Bullied

Ashley eyed her phone. It was almost ten o'clock at night. She was in her pajamas. Her English homework wasn't done. The class was reading *The Stranger*. It was by Albert Camus. Ashley loved the book.

But she couldn't think. Her mind kept straying to that stupid Snapchat picture. Now it was on Instagram too.

Darryl hadn't posted it. Melissa Avenal had. She was known as a tough girl. Melissa also had a temper. Ashley had never spoken to her. She figured Darryl had put her up to it.

Ashley stared at her English homework. There were three questions about *The Stranger*. She read them over and over. Her focus was shot. She checked Instagram again. There were only a few comments.

"She's stuck-up," one of them read.

Others just wanted to know why she was a snitch. "Who got in trouble?"

People thought she was guilty. That's what bothered her most. Nobody seemed to care that it wasn't true.

"Almost done?" her mom asked. She stood in the doorway. Mrs. Moore was still in her yoga gear. She tried to exercise every day.

"Yeah." Ashley looked at her. "Can I talk to you about something?"

"Sure," her mom said.

Ashley told her about Darryl. How he had taken a picture of her. That it was now online. How she was being labeled a snitch.

"I'm calling Dr. Stefani tomorrow," her mom said. "He's a great principal. He won't stand for this."

Dr. Stefani *was* a great principal. He was tall. His height was intimidating. He buzzed his brown hair extra short. The man had been a Marine. He was stern. But Dr. Stefani always listened.

Ashley thought he was nice. Dr. Stefani studied math after the military. He'd gotten his PhD. Then he taught. The principal really understood teenagers.

"Mom," Ashley said. "You can't. That'll just make things worse."

"I'm not going to let you be bullied."

"I need to figure this out. On my own."

Mrs. Moore stared at her daughter. Then she sighed.

"Okay," her mom said. "I guess I forgot who I was dealing with. You know you didn't do anything wrong. Remember that. Cheating is wrong. Turning in a cheater is not wrong."

"I know." Ashley turned back to her homework. "It's the accusation. I didn't do anything. Internet trolls try you without facts. I'm not guilty!"

"You're going to make a great lawyer someday."

"If I survive high school," Ashley said.

She barely slept that night. Thoughts about Darryl swirled in her head. That picture! What were kids saying about her?

Things were weird at school. Everybody had seen the picture. Ashley could tell. Kids looked at her funny. There was whispering.

Darryl wasn't in history that afternoon. He hadn't been in calculus either. Ashley was even more nervous. Did her mom go behind her back? Darryl would be in big trouble.

And it would be her fault. Again.

History ended. She overheard some students. Darryl was home sick.

Chapter 7
Target

Why is it taking so long?" Kayla asked. "My stomach is growling."

The girls were sitting in Adam's Burgers. It was a popular spot for students. They served cheap burgers, fries, and sandwiches.

"I don't know," Ashley said. "We haven't been here long."

She eyed their number on the table. It was 51.

They almost never hung out after school. The girls were too busy. Today, track and drama had been moved back an hour.

"Two other people got served. They came in after us," Kayla said. "We should leave."

"But we already paid," Ashley said.

At Adam's, customers paid before they ate. Then they were given a number. Numbers were called when the food was ready.

Kayla sometimes got impatient. When she was hungry, look out!

"Let's give them five more minutes," Ashley said.

"You're too nice," Kayla said, smiling. "You've got to be tough!"

The girls started laughing.

Then Ashley saw Skylar behind the counter. Did he work here? Oh no! She wouldn't have come if she'd known.

Skylar stood at the register. He smiled slightly. It wasn't a nice smile. He was messing with them. Was he the reason their food was taking so long?

Ashley lost her appetite. The thought of him near her food was gross. She didn't want to eat anything here.

"Let's bounce," she said.

"What about our food? We already paid." Kayla was confused.

"We'll go to Panda Express. I'll buy," Ashley said. She stood up. Kayla looked mad.

"But Panda's over in Walden Center."

"We'll be fine," Ashley said. "You already said we should leave. Come on."

Ashley walked out of Adam's. Kayla followed.

They moved quickly down the sidewalk. Cars passed by. They walked toward the other center. Ashley explained why she wanted to leave.

"We should have told the manager," Kayla said angrily. "Skylar should be fired."

"Yeah," Ashley said. "And then make him hate me more."

"Who cares what he thinks? He's not listening to you anyway. Nobody is."

Ashley loved her friend. She always gave it to her straight. Ashley knew she could count on her.

"I'm going to be late. Mr. Taylor is going to kill me," Kayla said. "We have to get our food to go."

"That's fine."

They got closer to the crosswalk. The two stood in front of Walden Center.

Melissa suddenly stepped out in front of them. She was taller than either girl. Her short blonde hair was pulled back.

"Well," she said. "If it isn't the snitch."

Ashley and Kayla stared at her.

"It's not cool to have a big mouth," Melissa said. "That can get you in trouble."

"What's your beef?" Kayla said.

"I didn't snitch," Ashley said.

They stared at one another. Right then, the signal light changed.

"Look," Ashley said. "I got 100 on that test. Why do I care if those guys cheated?"

"Later," Kayla said.

She hooked her arm around Ashley's. They walked past Melissa. Then the two girls crossed the street.

"You better watch it!" Melissa called.

"I can't believe those guys," Kayla said. They were halfway through the crosswalk. "They got Melissa to mess with you!"

"Just ignore her. Come on," Ashley said. She was a target now. But she had to stay above it.

Chapter 8
Bummed

Ashley's parents moved around the kitchen. Dinner prep was in full swing. Pasta night, yum! One of them would stir the sauce. The other would check on the noodles. Everyone kept an eye on the garlic bread.

Ashley and Marlon had set the table. Marlon was sitting at it. He was playing a game on his phone.

"Ashley," her father said. "I really think we should call the principal."

"You can't," Ashley said. She opened

the refrigerator. Ashley took out a pitcher of water. "That's what they're expecting me to do."

"But, honey," her mom said. "First they posted that picture. Now they're trying to pick fights."

"Melissa is a mean girl. She just said some dumb things," Ashley said. "Sticks and stones, right? Her words can't hurt me."

Everyone fell silent. Dinner smelled so good. The aroma of garlic and toasting bread filled the kitchen. Would the meal be ruined by a family fight?

Ashley hoped not. She was hungry now. The girls never went to Panda Express. The run-in with Melissa had wrecked their plan.

"Well," Marlon said, smiling. He looked

up from his game. "So much for Ashley rubbing off on those bad guys." Then he let out a big laugh.

Ashley walked by Marlon's room. "Hey," he called. "Ashley?" He was lying on his bed. YouTube was streaming on his tablet.

She stopped. Marlon was messy. His room was a disaster. It was filled with video games, books, and clothes. He liked it.

"What?" Ashley asked. "Are you going to laugh at me some more?"

"No," Marlon said. "You know I was just teasing."

"Yeah."

"What are you going to do?" Marlon seemed serious. Like he was actually worried about her.

"I don't know," she said. "I thought about a revenge post."

"Really?"

"Yeah, for like a half second. But that's lame. It's exactly what they did to me."

"Yeah," Marlon said. "It would probably feel good, though."

They stared at one another.

"It wouldn't be worth it," she said. "They would just do something else."

"You're smart," he said. "You've always been smarter about this stuff. I would have done something dumb."

"Well, I feel like a doormat. But I guess I'm doing the right thing. It just bugs me. Everybody assumes I told on them."

"I'll bet." Marlon sat up. He put his tablet down. "It was started by a bunch of losers."

"They're not losers," she said. "They tried to take a shortcut. But they got caught. Sometimes it's easier to blame someone. Then you don't have to take responsibility."

Ashley didn't want to be bitter. Most people were good, she thought. Darryl and his crew made her question that.

Chapter 9
Defense

Ashley worked in the student store once a month. All kids in student government did. The store sold school supplies and snacks. The merchandise was in the front. The register was in the back. The store was packed during lunch.

Today she worked with Shannon Cho. Shannon was freshman class president. They were ringing up the sales.

Mrs. Sturgess was the teacher in charge. She stood near the cash register.

"Thank you," Ashley said. She handed a student some change. The student had bought a folder and a bag of chips.

"What are you going to get, dude?" Nico asked. He was talking in an exaggerated voice.

Ashley looked in his direction. Nico and Darryl were looking at the drinks. The school only sold healthy drinks.

"I don't know." Darryl held up a drink. His tone was exaggerated too. "I don't want somebody telling my parents."

"Why, Darryl? Who would do that?"

"I don't know, Nico. Maybe somebody who likes to snitch."

Some of the students laughed. They looked at Ashley. How would she react?

Ashley stayed calm. She kept working.

Darryl and Nico walked up to the counter. They put their drinks in front of her.

"Don't tell anyone, Ashley," Darryl said. "Nothing bad about these."

Nico picked up his drink. He put the bottle close to her face. "See? It's not so bad," he said.

"It's blue," Darryl said.

"All right, out!" Mrs. Sturgess said. She moved over to them. "You boys are being rude."

"What?" Darryl whined.

"We were just playin'," Nico said.

They seemed surprised by the teacher. She was upset with them. It made Ashley feel good. They deserved to get in trouble.

"I don't care," Mrs. Sturgess said

firmly. "You're not acting like high school-ers. Leave, now."

Ashley knew what she needed to do. Getting kicked out of the student store was a big deal. It would only make those guys angrier. They deserved it. But it wouldn't matter. Ashley would still be a snitch. So she decided to step in.

"It's okay, Mrs. Sturgess," Ashley said. "We're friends."

Darryl and Nico eyed her. They looked surprised.

"Yeah, we're friends," Darryl said. "We were just kidding around."

"Ashley ..." Mrs. Sturgess said.

"Darryl and I are working on a project in history," Ashley said. "It's about the early 20th century. Prohibition. The guys were pretending. This store is like a nightclub. A speakeasy, right? One of the places Carry Nation didn't like. That is who we are studying."

"Yeah," Darryl said. "We were just doing that."

"Hmm, okay." Mrs. Sturgess went back to where she was standing. "Ring them up, I guess."

It was just before history. Darryl stood near Ashley. "Good looking out," Darryl said to her. "That was cool. You stuck up for us. I didn't think you would do that."

"Well, I didn't want to," she said. "You should think first. Before you post trash about people. Before you lie."

"Yeah," Darryl said sheepishly. "Sorry about that. I had Melissa take down the picture. It was stupid."

"Yeah, it was."

"Look, I'm sorry. We know the score now. Mrs. Smith told Mr. Raj we cheated. I guess we thought you told her."

"Why?" Ashley asked. "Why would I care?"

"You're always working so hard. You saw us. I thought you were looking down at us. Then I told you cheating was no big deal. You seemed bummed."

"I *was* bummed," Ashley said. "But I wouldn't tell on you. It's none of my business if you cheat."

They stared at each other.

"Well, I am sorry." Darryl tried to smile. "Look, we have to work together on our project. We might as well be friends, right?"

Ashley wanted to be mad. It would be easy to hold a grudge. But what would that solve?

"Okay," she said, smiling. "Maybe you can find some more pictures of Carry Nation. I'll work on the text."

"Cool."

They went into the classroom.

Chapter 10
New Friends

It's so weird, Kayla," Ashley said. "Darryl's really smart. He didn't need to cheat off Nico's test."

"He must not be that smart," Kayla said.

Ashley was walking to track practice. Kayla had drama rehearsal. She was doing a one-act play. It was about a student on exam day. Kayla was excited about it. Ashley knew it would be good. She thought her friend was a great actress.

Skylar and Nico were a few feet away. They walked right up to her. Had Darryl not said things were cool now?

"Hey," Nico said. "Thanks for helping me out at the student store."

"It was nothing," Ashley said.

"I was wondering," Skylar said. He looked at Nico. They smiled a bit.

Ashley started to get mad. Were they messing with her?

"Could you help me with calculus?" Skylar asked. "Nico is a bad tutor. And I don't want Darryl to know I need help."

Ashley stared at them. They stared back. The boys weren't smiling now. They were serious.

"Sure," Ashley said. Did this mean she was a nerd? She hoped it didn't show.

"See?" Nico said to Skylar. "I told you she'd say yes. Ashley's cool."

"Why do you want my help?"

Only hours before these guys were bullies. What had happened?

"You get perfect scores on your tests," Skylar said.

"Yeah," Nico said, laughing. "You're always doing things around school. Like those do-gooder clubs you're in. Those clubs make things better for people. I thought you'd be a good tutor. You seem really patient."

Ashley had been so upset. These dudes had been mean to her. Had they learned their lesson? She hoped so. Because Skylar needed her help. Helping people was what she was all about. She was in.

"Okay," she said. "We'll talk about it after class tomorrow."

She and Kayla continued walking.

"That was weird," Kayla said. "After everything they did? Why did you agree to help?"

"Well," Ashley said. "If I can help people, I should."

"Like I said, you're too nice." Kayla put her arm around her friend. They hugged.

Melissa suddenly appeared. She stared at Ashley. "Hey," she said quietly.

"Hi," Ashley said. Melissa made her nervous. But she smiled anyway.

"Are you going to yell at her again?" Kayla snapped.

"No," Melissa said. "I was going to ask a question. Will you help me in English?"

Ashley almost fell over. Was everyone

Mr. Moore rubbed his hands together. "Wow! Dinner smells so good," he said.

Mrs. Moore fake-sighed. "I cooked all day." And then she laughed.

Marlon and Ashley laughed too. The mood was light.

"So," Ashley said. "I have something to tell you."

Everyone looked at her.

"I was right. Sticks and stones may break my bones. But I killed my enemies with kindness. And you know what? They backed down. And now we're friends. They even want my help."

"Cool!" Marlon said. "You *did* rub off on them."

"Oh, honey," her mom said. "We're so proud of you. Your dad and I were ready to fight. But you held your ground. We trusted you to do the right thing."

"So it's settled?" her dad asked.

"Yes," Ashley said. "We're all moving on. I turned the other cheek. And those guys apologized. See? Most people *are* good."

"Sweet," Marlon said. "You rock."

"Thanks, dude," she said. "But I'll tell you something. No way do I want to go through that again. Words actually do hurt. It was hard not to lash out. But I did it. What a week!"